D1630202

N 0057066 4

BAGS OF TROUBLE

Andersen Young Readers' Library

Michael Harrison

BAGS OF TROUBLE

Illustrated by David McKee

Andersen Press · London

First published in 1988 by
Andersen Press Limited,
62-65 Chandos Place, London WC2

British Library Cataloguing in Publication Data
Harrison, Michael
  Bags of trouble.
  I. Title II. McKee, David, *1935-*
  823'.914 [J]
  ISBN 0-86264-219-1

Typesetting by Print Origination (NW) Limited, Formby, Liverpool
Printed and bound in Great Britain by Anchor Brendon Limited,
Tiptree, Essex

Contents

For Matthew

1
Troubled Jumble

It was the jumble sale that started the trouble. Matthew hadn't planned to waste a Saturday afternoon at school, but Miss Kirk had volunteered him into it.

'Now, children,' she had said to the class on Friday, 'I want four of you to help with the jumble sale tomorrow.'

Jennifer's hand had gone up almost before Miss Kirk had started speaking. She was the first to volunteer for anything.

'Thank you, Jennifer,' said Miss Kirk. 'Now, you know we're trying to collect money for a printer for our computer. The P.T.A. are collecting the jumble and setting the stalls up. I said that my class would supply some stewards.'

'What are stewarts, Miss?'

'Stew-arDs. Does anyone know what a steward is?'

It was then Matthew made his mistake.

'It's a dinner lady, Miss. They get all our

food and stew it 'ard.'

Miss Kirk nailed Matthew's mouth shut with one of her famous Looks.

'Thank you, Matthew. How suitable that the Computer Monitor should volunteer.'

'But, Miss . . . .'

'No buts, Matthew. Tomorrow you will be a steward. Now, we need two more.'

Matthew stared at the sheet of newspaper that covered the table he had been painting on. 'Government Health Warning' stared up at him in big letters: 'Cigarettes can damage your health.' They ought to put Government Health Warnings on more things, he thought. Miss Kirk for one, and my mouth for another. I'm always putting my foot in it.

GOVERNMENT HEALTH WARNING:
KEEP MOUTHS TIGHTLY SHUT
WHEN NEAR FEET.

And so, smouldering with resentment, Matthew reported to the school hall at two o'clock on a fine Saturday afternoon. As he

went through the door an amazing sight met him. The dinner tables were heaped with, well—with everything. As he looked around he saw that there was a pattern to it all. One table was covered in woollies, another in trousers, another in shoes. He started edging round to an interesting collection of games, Lego, and cars when—

'Ah, Matthew, over here please!'
came shooting its way across the hall like a grappling-hook. Miss Kirk had seen him. Matthew had just started making up a Government Health Warning: DANGER: TEACHERS' VOICES CAN . . . when a wall of boxes walked into him and toppled down leaving Kevin's mum looking like a surprised Humpty Dumpty surrounded by bricks.

'Sorry,' said Matthew.

Miss Kirk's voice shot across the hall. 'You'd better help Mrs Kinglock sort that out first.'

Kevin's mum smiled at him.

'Sorry, love. Kevin said you'd been caught for this. Just give me a hand with these odds and ends then.'

10

The cardboard boxes were filled with the sort of junk you see put out for the dustmen on Monday mornings. At first, the bins seem to be filled with wonders but when you look closely everything is cracked or chipped or missing one vital piece. The jumble looked the same.

In the bottom of one cardboard box Matthew found a cassette case. 'Mozart: Symphony 35—Haffner' it said.

'How much is this, Mrs Kinglock? It's my dad's birthday next week and he likes this sort of thing.'

'Slip it in your pocket, dear. We don't charge much, and you are helping.'

'Come on, Matthew,' called Miss Kirk. Jennifer stood smirking beside her, with Carol and Amy.

'Now, to begin with I want you, Matthew, to hold the doors open when we start at 2.30. Then, when the main rush is over, I want you to help people carry things to their cars. Go and wait by the doors until Mrs Worthing tells you to open them.'

Mrs Worthing was an anxious mum who should never have been allowed anywhere near a jumble sale. She clutched her handbag as if she thought everyone was trying to buy it. Matthew looked at it and wondered why she didn't have it grafted on. Perhaps one day women would evolve into a sort of kangaroo with a handbag growing out of one arm.

He turned from thoughts of winning the Nobel Prize for Medicine for his new technique of handbag transplants and glanced out of the door. He wished he hadn't. A regiment waited outside: determined faces, twitching hands, enormous shopping bags. Matthew could imagine them bursting through the door like a great wave breaking on the beach. Down he would go, over him would trample all those shoes—nervously he looked down, and again wished he hadn't—and moments later they would rush out again, this time weighed down by all the jumble laid out on the tables. He would end up dented like a golf-ball. DANGER: JUMBLE SALES CAN . . . but it was no good; this was beyond

joking about.

Matthew thought he could perhaps hide behind the door when it burst open. Then he remembered having *Flat Stanley* read to him in the Infants.

> GOVERNMENT HEALTH WARNING:
> DANGER: DOORS CAN DAMAGE
> YOUR WIDTH.

Matthew was brooding on the choice he faced—flat or dented—when he noticed the doorstop on the floor. The door could only open 90° so there was safety behind it. He stood poised, ready to sprint for that one safe spot, waiting for the entry of the vultures.

'Ah, David, splendid!' The voice of the Head.

'Yes, Miss,' he said. He had long ago given up saying, 'I'm Matthew.' It was safer if they didn't know your name. She swept on past him to the first group of mums.

'Ah, splendid! What an Aladdin's Cave! You have done well.'

Poor Aladdin, thought Matthew. Rub the lamp and end up with a table full of old handbags.

Then the Head seized the school bell and strode off through the door, leaving Mrs Worthing open-mouthed. A moment later the ringing of the bell was lost in the thundering of feet. If vultures could gallop, Matthew thought, this is what it would be like to die of thirst in the desert. No gentle circling overhead, but the sound of hooves getting closer and closer.

As he leant on the wall in his hiding place behind the door the sharp edge of the cassette case dug into him. He took it out to have a closer look. The outside looked clean enough to give as a present. Matthew opened it and took out the cassette. It was a C15 computer one.

'Matthew, help Mrs Craven with her bags, please,' came Miss Kirk's at-once-and-no-questions voice.

Mrs Craven was standing surrounded by plastic carrier-bags with 'It's clean—it's fresh—at Sainsbury's' printed in orange on the outside. What was inside the bags looked neither clean nor fresh. Matthew picked up two of the bags and followed Mrs Craven out to the playground. She led him to a bicycle leaning against a wall. It had enormous baskets on both front and back. Obviously a special jumble sale model, Matthew thought. They ought to make specialist bikes: a going-to-school model that would break down within the first hundred metres; a going-fishing model whose seat took off and turned into a stool to sit on and whose cross-bar held telescopic rods; a model . . . but by this time Mrs Craven had managed to stuff her carrier-bags precariously into her baskets. She smiled vaguely at Matthew and wobbled down the drive with 'It's clean' unconvincingly sticking up behind her.

Matthew decided he could not face the hall again and slunk down the passage to the toilets, not that he could be sure of being safe from Miss Kirk's radar even there. As he passed his classroom he saw her coat hanging off the back of her chair.

'I could sneak that into the jumble,' he thought. 'That would teach her.'

Michael went into his classroom and picked up Miss Kirk's coat. He could imagine some really large and frightening mother standing there with the coat in her hands and saying to a quivering Miss Kirk: 'I have paid good money for this garment. My Gladys is playing Cinderella in the school panto and this will do just right for her rags—if I mend it up a bit.'

Then Matthew had another picture, this time of Miss Kirk turning round slowly and looking straight at *him*. He chucked the coat down again. Miss Kirk's keys fell out of a pocket on to the floor, her school keys, the key for the computer room.

2
Software Solution

The computer room was really a broom cupboard. There had been a panic about locking the computer up after some local schools had had theirs stolen. The P.T.A. had arranged a working party and decorated the broom cupboard, put in electric sockets, an extractor fan that worked off the light switch to keep the air fresh, and a bench. The room was next door to Matthew's class so Miss Kirk was sort of in charge, and so she had a key, and Matthew was Computer Monitor this term. He knew more about it than most of the teachers anyway.

Matthew picked up the keys slowly. It would be best to know what was on the tape. Perhaps it was a very short Mozart symphony. Perhaps it was blank. Perhaps it was a brilliant game that would make the next hour pass more quickly.

He looked carefully out of the door. No one was in sight. There was a roar like lions having

a hymn practice coming from the hall, but everywhere else was quiet. He walked quickly to the computer room door, put the key in, turned it, opened the door, went in and closed it behind him. It was completely dark and completely silent. He paused, listening for sounds of pursuit. Nothing.

He put his hand out and switched the light on. The faint purr of the fan broke the silence and was comforting. There was a wide shelf down one side of the little room. Three stools were pushed tidily under it. On the bench was the monitor, tape-recorder, and the BBC computer.

Matthew switched on at the wall and slid the cassette into the recorder. He pulled the middle stool out and sat down in front of the monitor. He turned up the volume on the tape recorder and pressed PLAY.

There was a moment's silence as the white leader tape unwound, followed by a continuous high note. The air-raid warning, Miss Kirk called it. Then came short buzzes with more whine in between. So, it *was* computer tape, and it *did* have a program on it. Was it a BBC program?

Matthew rewound the tape and typed 'CHAIN' on the computer. 'Searching' appeared on the screen, then 'Loading PLAN' followed by the hex numbers. The computer bleeped to say it was ready. A menu appeared on the screen. Matthew looked at it:

*S*chools

*H*ardware

*D*ates

it said. He tried typing 'S'. The screen changed. It was now filled with a list of schools. Matthew recognised most of them from the school's football league. There, number 3, was his own: Bainton Road Junior. He typed '3'. The screen then read:

BAINTON ROAD JUNIOR

HARDWARE: one BBC B

    One colour monitor

    One BBC data recorder

LOCATION: enter school, turn left, then right. 2nd door on left. Chubb lock.

DATES: 8 October Jumble Sale
     10 May: 50/50 Auction
     21 June: Summer Fête

Matthew looked at it, bewildered. DAN-GER: COMPUTERS CAN TAKE OVER THE WORLD. Why store so much useless information? He remembered his dad going on about having to fill in so many pointless forms. Perhaps whoever was in charge wanted information about computers and Saturday P.T.A. activities. But why?

Matthew typed 'S' and got back to the list of schools. He selected the next on the list—Bishop Corben Junior—because they had had their computer stolen a few weeks ago. There was the same sort of list but at the bottom was the one word 'STOLEN'.

Matthew sat and stared at the screen. Then he looked at other schools, then at the lists of hardware, and then at the list of dates. He sat and thought again.

After a few minutes he got up and switched the light off. He opened the door carefully.

Nobody was in sight. He slipped quietly next door. Under his classroom's paint-trolley was a pile of old newspapers. He went quickly through the pile and pulled out all the copies there were of the local weekly paper. He took them back into the computer room and went through them carefully. Every few minutes he typed something on the keyboard and checked the monitor screen.

It took about twenty minutes, but then he was certain. There had been five thefts of computers from schools reported in the local paper. Each of these schools was on the tape. Each had 'STOLEN' printed on the bottom of its list. Each had been stolen at a weekend when there was an event listed on the tape. Bishop Corben had lost theirs the same weekend as their P.T.A. barn dance.

Matthew thought hard. Someone was stealing school equipment. Sometimes a monitor went, but it was usually just the computer itself. Matthew looked at the BBC computer. It would just about fit into a carrier bag—it's clean, it's fresh, it's stolen from school. They were stolen when schools were full of strangers, strangers who could wander a bit in the school, as long as they didn't lurk suspiciously, as long as they knew where they were going and what they wanted. What they wanted—perhaps they stole to order? Walking out with a bag full of jumble was the perfect cover . . . .

He got off his stool quickly and turned the light off to shut out the noise of the fan. Nothing. He locked the door and put the light on again. The cassette must have been sent to the jumble sale by mistake. The crook must have kept it in the Mozart box to hide it. Someone—wife, mother—must have had a clear-out. Sooner or later he would find it had gone. He would need to get it back before anyone tried it on a computer. His wife or mother would tell him where the jumble sale was. The Head would send him to Mrs Kinglock. Mrs Kinglock would send him to Matthew. What would Matthew say? What would he do to Matthew?

'Don't take cassettes from strangers,'

groaned Matthew. He must take it back to Mrs Kinglock. He must tell her he'd remembered his dad had got that one, pretend he hadn't opened the cassette box.

'But what happens when this computer's stolen?' he thought. 'I can't just let him get away with it. I wish there was a famous four more of me or another secret six here.'

Matthew didn't believe that policemen sit about in police stations just waiting for small boys to turn up with the latest information on international criminals. He pictured himself walking into the local police station. Daniel's dad was the sergeant there. He wouldn't be very pleased to see Matthew after the trouble with the guy last year. It might be all right in a book but he couldn't do it. His throat would go dry, he'd stutter and look silly and Sergeant Morton would tell him to run along, and he'd tell Daniel again how daft his friend Matthew was.

He could tell the Head. He could just picture that, too.

'Ah, er, Henry dear! You've got something

to show me? How lovely! Yes, I'll look in a minute just as soon as I've done these swimming certificates. Don't worry!' And she'd put the cassette down and lose it. Matthew could still remember her sitting on his Viking longship when he was in the Infants. Or she'd try to load it and press RECORD and PLAY and wipe the lot. She liked showing visitors the computer room, but she didn't understand it at all.

Wipe it? Could he wipe it himself and then give it back to Mrs Kinglock? No, because then the crook would know that he knew—and anyway he might have a back-up tape. A back-up! Matthew knew that this was what he must do. He must make a copy and then he could return the original and have time to think what he should do. He took his own private cassette from the shelf and carefully copied the program on side two.

He put the two boxes into his pocket, switched everything off, and left the room as carefully as he had entered it. He put Miss Kirk's keys back and tidied away the newspapers. All the time he worried about how he could tell someone about the tape without getting into trouble for taking the keys.

Then Matthew had a brainwave. He got out the newspapers again and found a pair of scissors on Miss Kirk's desk. He cut out all the reports of computer thefts in the local paper. He found an old envelope on Miss Kirk's desk and put the cuttings and computer tape

inside. He crossed out the Head's name and address and was just about to write: 'Police: look at this!' on the outside when he paused. He suddenly had a picture of the whole school having to sit down and copy 'Police: look at this!' off the board while the Head paced up and down to check the handwriting.

She would suddenly seize Matthew's piece of paper with a triumphant cry and he would be forced to stumble out to the front and explain in increasingly unconvincing words why he had sent a Mozart symphony to Sergeant Morton in an envelope padded out with bits of newspaper. He searched desperately through the paper until he found a headline: POLICE REPORT MORE DOING TON ON BY-PASS.

He carefully cut out letters and Pritt-sticked them on to the envelope:

P O L I C E

S E R G E A N T   M O R T O N

He looked at the letters that were left: PORDOIONBYPS. He tried to think of some useful message that he could make with them but he had never been good at 'Scrabble' and so he regretfully threw them away.

He put the envelope into Daniel Morton's drawer and then took it out again. He didn't want Daniel playing amateur detective. He'd find some way of delivering it himself. He put it into his own drawer for the moment. After the jumble sale was over he'd come back and get it.

He slipped back into the hall and edged round to Mrs Kinglock's table.

'Hello, love,' she said. 'Miss Kirk's been looking for you. I told her you were probably helping in the car-park.'

'Thanks,' said Matthew. 'Has anyone else been asking about me?'

'No, love. Should they have?'

'No, I just wondered. Oh, I remembered. This cassette, my dad's got it already so I'll just put it back. You'll probably sell it to someone else.' (Someone else might work it out, he thought. But who else would bother, they'd just chuck it away.)

'Oh well, I'm sorry about that, dear.'

Matthew felt a hand on his shoulder.

3
Too Many Good Turns

Matthew turned round. Miss Kirk had her don't-panic-I'm-in-charge look.

'Matthew, Jennifer is feeling unwell. Could you please see her home? I can't leave here, and it's not far.'

'All right.' Matthew was relieved: no questions about where he had been, and he could get away before the cassette owner arrived.

'That's a good boy. Just fetch her bag from the classroom, will you?'

As Matthew crossed the hall again he looked at the women picking over the jumble. Their hands had slowed down and they were even talking to each other. Matthew pictured well-fed vultures chatting over the remains of breakfast. How useful if real vultures could have detachable stomachs like these carrier-bags. He saw a pair of wellingtons sticking out of a blue-and-white bag labelled 'Boots'. The vultures would carry bags with 'Guts' printed on them. He tried to think what the vulturine equivalent of 'It's clean, it's fresh' would be.

The bag was on Miss Kirk's desk. It sat there bulging. Perhaps bags are really a form of alien life, Matthew thought. They landed from a flying suitcase at night and are trying to take over the world. Handbags clamp on to women's wrists and hitch a ride to where they want to go—mainly Sainsbury's. There they give instructions to the carrier-bags. DANGER: HANDBAGS CAN CONTROL YOUR SHOPPING.

Jennifer's bag was a zip-up sports bag coloured like a battery, a free offer if you bought enough batteries to light up an entire street. Miss had one too. Jennifer always liked to copy Miss.

At least it was light, Matthew thought, as he picked it up. He knew what was in it. Jennifer had volunteered to take the painting overalls home for her mother to wash.

Jennifer was sitting in the entrance hall under the Swiss-cheese plants and the mobile of the planets the Infants had made, looking greenly pale.

'I feel sick,' she said when Matthew appeared. 'You'll have to carry my bag. I feel awful.'

'Do you think you're going to be sick?'

'I expect so,' she said. 'I'm sick a lot. Mum says she's never known anybody to be as sick as me.'

'Come on, then,' he said.

'Ah, Carol dear, and James dear,' said the Head. 'Take this letter and hand it in at the police station on your way home, please. I

thought it was time that Sergeant Morton came to talk about the Yellow Triangle Code again.'

'Green, Miss,' said Jennifer, 'and Cross.'

'No, no,' said the Head. 'It's Sergeant Morton. Sergeant Green was here before. I never forget a name. And Sergeant Morton isn't cross at all, he's very kind. You must never be afraid of the police, dear.'

Matthew realised that Jennifer really must be feeling ill when she just said, 'Yes, Miss,' instead of arguing. He took the letter and slipped it into his trouser pocket.

Jennifer seemed to feel better when she got into the open air and walked briskly. In fact, Matthew had difficulty keeping up.

'I thought you were feeling sick?'

'No, I just got fed up with being stuck in there.'

'Then why did you volunteer?' Matthew asked.

'It's my mum. She's always on at me about doing well at school and she's always coming up to see Miss Kirk. I get my own back by badgering Miss for jobs.'

'I don't see how that gets your own back,' said Matthew.

'Well, Miss daren't say anything nasty about me to Mum because she thinks I'm really trying hard. In fact it drives her mad really. Do you remember when I tidied her cupboard one playtime? It looked lovely, but she couldn't find anything for days. It was much more fun than skipping in the playground. And every time I put anything away for her, or tidy up, I put things in a slightly different place.'

'DANGER,' thought Matthew, 'TIDY CHILDREN CAN LOSE YOUR SANITY.'

'She only asks for volunteers now when she's not thinking. I have to guess what needs doing and volunteer before she can ask anybody else.'

'But isn't it boring, doing all the jobs?'

'Well, yesterday I cleared up all the ink that Martin spilt while you were doing long division. It took me a long time so I didn't do any maths. Miss can't tell my mum I couldn't do the sums.'

'But you looked so ill,' Matthew said.

'Reflection. Hold something pale in your lap, like white paper, and sit in the right light and you can fool everyone. They don't really look at you.'

Matthew was amazed at this superbrain and was just going to tell Jennifer about the computer cassette when Mrs Craven called to them from the other side of the road.

'Oh, Matthew, do you understand about chains? Mine's come off and I can't seem to get it on.'

The jumble-bike was propped against a lamp-post. Its massive baskets gaped open like the mouths of baby birds in a nest waiting for their worms. Matthew expected them to be cheeping and crying until Mrs Craven fed them again with a nice fat juicy carrier-bag.

Mrs Craven had managed to get the chain well wrapped round the pedal. By the time Matthew had fixed it his hands and trousers were well oiled.

'You are a lamb,' Mrs Craven said. 'I'm just

popping back to the jumble sale to check I haven't missed any bargains. It's not over yet, is it?'

'Oh no, Mrs Craven,' said Jennifer, 'I had to come away with Matthew because Miss Kirk asked him to buy the oranges for our football match tomorrow. I had to come because he couldn't manage to carry the oranges and the painting overalls,' and she pointed to the bag Matthew had been carrying.

'I'll tell Justin,' said Mrs Craven, getting back on the jumble-bike. 'He's playing tomorrow. He'll be glad to hear about the oranges. He's always complaining he gets thirsty. Goodbye now, and thanks so much, Matthew.'

'Why did you have to say that?' Matthew asked as soon as the rear basket was out of earshot.

'I couldn't tell her I felt ill, could I? She'd ask my mum if I felt better.'

'But what are we going to do about the oranges?'

'Buy some, of course. Mrs Wootton gave me

a pound for helping. We'll only need six oranges for both teams. Come on!'

Matthew lay in bed that evening listening to the rain falling on the window, the television muttering away to itself, and the washing machine clicking and grinding in the kitchen. His mother had not been very pleased when he came home with oil on his trousers. She had put them straight into the washing machine, risking a hot wash to get them clean. He hoped that the rain would ease off so that they could play tomorrow. As he thought about the day he remembered the envelope with the cassette in it. He'd left it in his drawer. Oh well, it would have to wait until Monday now. Did the police work on Sundays? He mustn't forget anything else—the oranges, for example. He had put them down in the kitchen, on the washing machine. The washing machine! His trousers, going round and round! The Head's letter going round and round in his trousers in the washing machine! The Head's letter getting soggier and soggier going round and round in his trousers in the washing machine. The ink on the Head's soggy letter running in steady streams off the paper into the water of the washing machine. The Head's message being carried out to sea with the waste water and being laid down at the bottom of the ocean. It would become fossilised and wait millions of years for earth movements to bring it up to the surface again. Children on a school trip would see the letters in the rock and dig them out very carefully one by one. The colours from the painting overalls that Jennifer had taken home might end up in the same rocks . . . .

Matthew fell asleep quite cheerfully. The Head would never remember that she had written. If she did she wouldn't remember his name. And tomorrow was Sunday, and football, and nothing would go wrong . . . .

4
It's in the Bag

Sunday morning dawned bright and sunny; Matthew's mum didn't. He was spooning his Special K (for extra energy) into his mouth when his mother started emptying the washing machine. The clothes were flecked with white as if it had been snowing inside the machine. She turned round and faced him over the cereal packets.

'How many times,' she shouted very quietly, so as not to wake his dad who was having a lie-in, 'have I told you about leaving paper tissues in your trouser pockets? I've got to do this whole load again now.'

Matthew realised that this was one of those questions to which there is no answer. Any number he said would be called cheek, and 'I don't know' would be worse. He thought it was probably seventeen but he wasn't quite sure. He decided to play safe.

'Sorry, Mum.'

'And I expect you'll come home covered in

mud after your match. It was pouring all night. It'll be knee-deep in mud.'

Matthew opened his mouth to say that if it was knee-deep then no one could play football because they wouldn't be able to find the ball, but fortunately he thought better of it.

'Here's your kit, then.'

'I don't need a top, Mum. We've got our new team shirts today.'

'Just don't come home with any mud on the clothes you're wearing. You'll need them for school tomorrow now you've messed up my washing. I'd like to know what goes on inside your head sometimes.'

Matthew pictured people with monitor screens on their foreheads or computer print-out coming out of their ears.

'What are you grinning for now? Get off, or you'll be late.'

Matthew picked up his kit, and at the last moment remembered the oranges. He grabbed the brown paperbag off the kitchen table, nearly knocking a milk bottle over as he did so. He went out of the back door, up the side passage and jumped over the gate to save time. As he ran off down the pavement towards the football field he heard his mum shouting some last minute threat or good wishes after him but he ignored her. He didn't want to be late. As he ran he made up newspaper stories about his triumphs in the match: 'MATTHEW THE MARVEL' the headline would read. 'This slim, fair-haired footballing wonder-child made his opponents look like complete beginners. This great athlete may play for England in the next World Cup if Scotland Yard can spare him from his role as private investigator into the international computer stealing conspiracy.'

There was quite a crowd on the football field. This was the first match the school team would play in their new shirts. The P.T.A. had organised a Sponsored Kick to raise the money. It looked as though all those who had contributed had turned up to see the new shirts in action. They stood around in the sunshine talking and laughing. The other team had changed already and were kicking a ball around. They looked large, and good. The Bainton Road team stood trying to look quietly confident while they waited for Miss Kirk to turn up with the shirts.

Matthew wondered what would happen if Miss Kirk didn't arrive. He couldn't play in his clean clothes. His mum would get really mad if he did. He couldn't play without a top on, not in front of all those parents, and the girls.

Jennifer came out of a huddle of girls towards him.

'Did you remember the oranges, Matthew?'

He took the brown paperbag out and handed it to her.

'It's a good thing I thought of bringing a knife and a plate,' she said. 'I'd better not cut them up until half-time, or they'll dry up. I'll bring them out—I might as well get the credit for wasting my money on you lot.'

Just then Miss Kirk's blue Fiesta drove in through the gate and parked next to the pavilion. She got briskly out, followed by a man in a duffle-coat who had a shiny black bag hanging from one shoulder. Has she brought

a doctor, Matthew wondered. Are the other side that good?

'Sorry to be a little late,' she called out. 'I've brought Mr Lathbury along. He's the reporter on the local paper and he's agreed to take some pictures of our team in their new shirts.'

'Strips,' said Kevin.

'Not here,' said Miss Kirk. 'Change in the pavilion as usual. Matthew, fetch my bag from the car, please. It's on the back seat.'

Matthew carried Miss Kirk's battery-bag over to the pavilion. She smiled vaguely at him as she made her way over to the parents waiting on the sideline. Mr Lathbury was busy taking things out of his bag, but not too busy to smile cheerfully around. I wonder if that's her boyfriend, Matthew thought. He didn't have time to think about it any longer because a shout of: 'Come on, Matthew! We want to get changed,' came from the pavilion.

'Some pavilion,' Matthew thought. 'Some people have bigger garden sheds.' He went into the wooden building and put the bag down. Kevin Beechcroft's big hands shot out and unzipped it. One hand went in—

'Hey, what on earth . . . ?'

Eleven mouths dropped open as the contents of the bag appeared. Painting overalls. Painting overalls made out of men's shirts. Painting overalls needing a good wash in Jennifer's mum's washing machine. Well-painted painting overalls.

Matthew shut his mouth firmly. He knew

just what had happened, but he wasn't going to say anything. Miss Kirk's battery-bag would be sitting next to the washing machine. Jennifer's battery-bag was sitting in the middle of twenty-two pairs of feet, looking in considerable danger.

'Major victory for bag conspirators,' thought Matthew. 'Bag 007 fools opposition.'

'Come along!' called Miss Kirk. 'Everyone's waiting for you.'

'But, Miss—it's the wrong bag.'

'Right, you'll have to wear your old shirts.'

'But, Miss, I didn't bring mine.'

'Nor did I.'

'Nor me.'

'Then you'll have to wear one of these.'

The Bainton Road Junior School football team slunk out of the pavilion dressed in boots, socks, shorts—and painting overalls.

There was silence.

Mr Lathbury smiled even more than usual and quickly took some photographs. Miss Kirk was, as usual, quite calm.

'A slight hitch,' she said firmly, glaring at

Jennifer. 'Our new shirts will be worn officially at school next week—and Mr Lathbury will come to school to photograph them.'

'I'd love to, Cathy,' said Mr Lathbury, 'just let me know when.'

The first half was not a great success for Bainton Road Juniors. Feeling silly didn't improve their play. At half-time they were 5-0 down and Miss Kirk strode on to the pitch with her right-let's-have-no-more-of-this-nonsense look. Jennifer trotted behind clutching her paperbag, knife, and plate.

'This is a disgrace—Oh, what is it now, Jennifer?'

'Please, Miss, I bought some oranges for the teams.'

'Oh, very well. Share them out. Not that this lot deserve any—and then I'll have a few words with them. I'll call the Bishop Corben linesman over to collect theirs.'

The two plates were held up, and Jennifer tipped the bag. Out rolled six golden-brown—onions. In a moment of horror Mat-

51

thew saw the brown paperbag that Jennifer should have been holding sitting on top of the washing machine at home. DANGER: THESE BAGS ARE DANGEROUS. DO NOT FEED.

Miss Kirk spoke very quietly.

'Jennifer, is there some simple explanation for this?'

'I don't know, Miss. Matthew bought them. I was ill you remember. He took me home and said he would buy them.'

Twenty-five pairs of eyes looked at Matthew. The spectators were probably looking at him too but fortunately they were too far away to see what was happening. Matthew felt himself going as red as a fine patch of paint he remembered Kevin decorating the painting shirt with last week.

'I-I must have picked up the wrong bag.'

'There seem to have been rather too many wrong bags this morning,' Miss Kirk said. 'But perhaps that is why your mother is just coming through the gate. I didn't think she was a keen football fan.'

Matthew's mum rushed up, holding out the brown paperbag of oranges. She looked smart and she smiled round.

'Good morning, Miss Kirk. I'm afraid I sent Matthew off with the wrong bag this morning. I only realised when I started to cook the dinner so I came straight round with your oranges.'

Miss Kirk smiled back. 'Thank you so much for bringing them. Perhaps they will revive the team's skills. Matthew obviously needs practice in bag-carrying. He can look after my bag when we go to the museum tomorrow.'

5
Monday Mummies

Monday morning was wet again. The steady stream of rain did nothing to raise Matthew's spirits as he walked to school. He had to do something about the cassette before more computers were stolen. Some brilliant detective work would stop him thinking about Sunday. In fact, the whole weekend had been awful altogether. If he could only travel back in time to just before that silly joke on Friday so that everything would have turned out differently. You ought to be able to watch edited highlights of a selection of weekends and then choose the one you wanted. The trouble was, it would be like library books. The pushy people would end up with the good weekends, the Roald Dahl ones, and he'd end up with . . . .

'Wait for me, Matthew!'

Jennifer—all he needed to complete his misery. If they saw him walk through the gate with her they'd all think the mix-up with the bags was a joke they'd planned together.

'Matthew! Wait! I want you to give Miss a message for me.'

Matthew waited. Raindrops dripped from his nose. Perhaps he would dissolve away like a sugar lump.

Jennifer came up, out of breath and out of temper. 'Why couldn't you wait?'

'Sorry, it's wet.'

'Look, I've forgotten the football shirts and Miss will be even more cross. I'm going back for them. I may be a bit late so explain, will you?'

'We're leaving at nine for the museum,' Matthew reminded her.

'That's all right, then. The bus goes past my house. I'll get on at that stop. Tell Miss I'll see her on the bus. Bye!'

Matthew stood looking after her. Miss Kirk would not be pleased. She liked to have everyone together when she called the register so that she could improve them with a few well-chosen criticisms. She was not going to be pleased to see him to start with. He turned and splashed on his way.

In fact, Miss Kirk was surprisingly cheerful. It was the jumble sale's success in breaking all records and the Head's enthusiasm. She had stopped Miss Kirk on her way into school and thanked her for her help, and for arranging for that very sensible boy Matthew to help Mrs Craven with her problems. It seemed that Mrs Craven had been most complimentary about it. Would Miss Kirk please thank Matthew for her.

So Miss Kirk passed on the Head's thanks to Matthew for helping Mrs Craven with her bags and her bicycle chain. Jennifer, in her absence, came in for most of the blame for Sunday.

'I know she means to be helpful,' Miss Kirk said, 'but so often she just makes things worse. I can't find a thing in my cupboard now. She needs someone level-headed like you to keep an eye on her.'

Matthew wondered how a flat head would help him control Jennifer. Miss Kirk was always saying she had eyes in the back of her head—though what use could they be under all that hair—and perhaps she expected him to have eyes in the top of his head. They wouldn't see much, not on a flat head.

He took the envelope with the cassette out of his desk and slipped it into his anorak pocket. There might be a chance to drop it into the police station.

Miss Kirk called the register quickly, and gave Matthew a bag containing thirty clipboards. His knees buckled under the weight.

'I said you needed practice. Now do try to get them to the museum.'

Matthew thought he would end up permanently bent sideways from the weight of the bag. He wouldn't be able to go through doorways forwards because his head would bang on the wall. If he forgot and ran through his head could be knocked off completely.

Matthew took a look round his classroom in case he never came back. He suddenly felt that he might miss it. The windows looked out over the school field and Miss Kirk's geraniums glowed bright red against the distant green of the grass. The room was tidy, the chairs

pushed neatly under the blue-topped tables, a pile of books in each place waiting quietly for their return. The walls were bright with their Egyptian paintings with Kevin's red Nile for the story of Moses and the plagues clashing badly with the geraniums.

'Come on, Matthew, do keep up,' Miss Kirk said, shattering his nostalgia at once. 'We mustn't miss this bus. There isn't another one for an hour.'

'Come on! Keep together! Keep up! Let's have a nice crocodile now!'

Matthew was not the only one who pictured Miss Kirk's nice crocodile. The whole of the class walked behind Miss opening and shutting their mouths. Fortunately the clicking of twenty-nine sets of teeth was covered by the traffic noise.

The bus driver didn't seem very cheerful either as Miss Kirk ordered her flock on to the bus, each crocodile holding out 20p for the fare.

'Upstairs!' she said. 'We'll let the elderly sit downstairs, and we can notice things to write about later.'

'Just a moment,' said the driver. 'Are you paying?'

Miss Kirk's Look didn't seem to work on bus drivers. She paid her 40p and went up the stairs to stop the squabbling over seats.

The most interesting thing to notice on the journey to write about later was Jennifer's mother. She was panicking round the bus stop. Jennifer stood quite calmly, the battery-bag at her feet, while her mother seemed to be turning in small circles and talking non-stop, like a clockwork toy going wrong. DANGER: DO NOT OVERWIND THIS MOTHER, thought Matthew.

As the bus approached she had her arm up and down like an agitated ostrich's neck and almost before the doors opened she was on the bus and off again.

'It's not the right bus, Jennifer. They're not on it. You must have got it wrong. It's the wrong day. They're going by coach. They caught the earlier bus. They're going this afternoon.'

'Mrs Polstead,' came Miss Kirk's voice. 'We are upstairs.'

'Oh, Miss Kirk, I am so glad. I am so sorry. I will collect the overalls. Do have a nice. Do behave your. Do.' And the bus doors closed, leaving her standing on the pavement with her mouth still going up and down. Matthew wondered if she would still be there when they

came back. Perhaps she would have run down and would have to stay there until someone came along and wound her up again.

Miss Kirk must have felt sorry for Jennifer because she didn't tell her off at all but went back to pointing out interesting things like lamp-posts.

The museum was an imposing-looking building rather more like a prison than anything else. Its windows were barred and a closed-circuit television camera watched the door. Miss Kirk gathered her class around her and tried to fix them all with a Look simultaneously.

'Right. Listen. We. Are. Going. To. Be. On. Our. Best. Behaviour. At. All. Times. In. The. Museum. No running. No eating. No shouting. Anything you thought of doing—don't. Right, we'll go in now QUIETLY.'

They went into the entrance hall of the museum. Racks of picture-postcards, guidebooks, tea-towels, and Christmas cards rose up on both sides. In the middle of the hall was a small display case containing the museum's latest treasures. Each new item they acquired went first into a special display here.

The curator looked almost pleased to see them. He was a mild man by nature but years of school parties had made him both bald and grey, and rather short-tempered. But Miss Kirk's classes were always quiet, well-behaved, and even interested in what they had come to see. He knew he had nothing to worry about.

Miss Kirk gathered her class round the special display case.

'Here are some pieces of Roman pottery found in the excavations for the new Sainsbury's,' she said. 'When you go shopping there next year you will be able to think of the Roman feet that . . . .'

She seemed to lose interest in what she was saying. The class followed her gaze. A double-decker bus had stopped at the end of the road. The driver was leaning out of the door waving frantically and holding up the bag of clipboards. Matthew went cold. 'I wonder if

they'd have me here as an exhibit,' he thought. 'Case 65: Bainton Road Junior School Pupil. Believed to be the only child turned to stone by a teacher's Look.'

'It's all right, Miss Kirk,' said the curator. 'I'll go and collect it. You carry on.'

'Thank you very much,' she said, and sighed deeply as if she had all the world's cares on her shoulders. 'Now, when we get our clipboards—*if* we get our clipboards—we do *not* lean them on display cases. You can easily scratch the glass with the clips. Nor do you lean on the display cases like this.'

Miss Kirk put her elbows on the glass and leant forwards. The extra weight of the world's worries was too much. Her elbows went through the glass and shattered it. Fortunately she was wearing a coat because of the rain and so was unhurt.

Unfortunately, breaking a glass case set off the alarm system. Bells rang out as if it was the end of every lesson at once. The museum door quivered briefly as it locked automatically.

'Don't panic,' said Miss Kirk, 'we will continue with our visit. You will have to manage without clipboards while the curator sorts this out. This way, please.'

The curator stood outside, helplessly clutching thirty clipboards. The doors were locked against him. The controls were inside. Bells rang. The siren of an approaching police car grew louder and nearer. Miss Kirk talked about Egyptian mummies.

6
An Open and Shut Case

The best thing about Egyptian mummies, Matthew thought, was that they were so bandaged up that they couldn't say anything. They couldn't hear anything either.

Apart from the ringing of the alarm-bells, they had had a peaceful visit to the museum. Miss Kirk had talked about each display case and had then given out the questionnaires. Matthew had listened carefully in case she suddenly asked him a question and so he could fill in the blanks without looking at the exhibits. They all had to write on the floor as they didn't have any clipboards. Matthew looked round at the twenty-nine bottoms sticking up in the air. He wasn't sure whether they looked more like animals grazing or a team of detectives searching the scene of the crime for clues. Miss Kirk looked at him as if she knew what crime had been committed and who had committed it.

He settled down to drawing his favourite

mummy, the pharaoh's pet cat, and listened to the row that was developing nicely in the museum hall. There was one thing about Miss Kirk, he thought. No one could ever put her in the wrong.

'I shall be reporting the incident to the Health and Safety Inspectorate,' she was saying in her wake-up-at-the-back-and-listen voice. 'It's a mercy one of my pupils wasn't cut to ribbons. You have a duty to make sure the museum is safe.'

The curator's feeble suggestion that the cases weren't designed as elbow rests merely fuelled her scorn.

'People always do silly things. You should know that. And it needed no weight at all to shatter that glass. What if I had been a great heavy man? Would it have gone right through the floor?'

The curator decided to retreat and went to take a long time finding a dustpan and brush. This left Miss Kirk free to turn on Sergeant Morton, who had arrived in the police car.

'I really cannot understand why it took you

so long to get here, Sergeant. There are many valuable items in this museum. The thieves could be miles away by now.'

Sergeant Morton tried to explain that it wasn't usual for there to be a two-mile traffic jam. He said, patiently, several times, that a bus had stopped for about ten minutes opposite a parked car, blocking the main road in both directions. Miss Kirk wisely refused to be sidetracked by buses. Matthew wisely decided that this wasn't the moment to give Sergeant Morton his envelope.

'And when you *do* get here, you don't have the emergency keys and have to return to the police station to fetch them. Police cars should carry all the necessary keys. Suppose a case had fallen on some poor child and cut him badly. He could be lying in pools of blood for hours while you drive up and down all morning.'

Her eyes met Matthew's and he could see *which* child she would like to see lying under the mummies while the ambulance crew waited helplessly outside the locked doors,

69

improvising a stretcher out of thirty clipboards.

Sergeant Morton decided to go and sort out the traffic jam. Some American tourists who stopped him outside and asked him the way to the museum were surprised at his answer.

'I thought English policemen were so polite and helpful,' one said. 'I'm glad he wasn't carrying a gun.'

Miss Kirk had so cowed the curator that he gave everyone change for pound coins when they bought eightpenny postcards, without a murmur.

The crocodile made its way quietly back to the bus stop. When the Number 30 drew up the driver looked even less cheerful than he had earlier. Fortunately they all had the right change after buying their postcards, and Miss Kirk remembered to pay too.

'Now, Matthew,' she said as she settled down with a small sigh of relief, 'please don't leave the clipboards on the bus again.'

Matthew thought that this was probably his worst moment.

'Right! Wait here!' ordered Miss Kirk and positively ran down the stairs. 'Just a moment!' she said to the bus driver. Then she remembered her dignity and walked back towards the museum and the bag of clip-boards.

Matthew had followed her downstairs nervously and so he saw the bus driver's sudden smile. As Miss Kirk went round the corner the bus doors closed with a swish and the bus pulled quietly out from the pavement. The driver was humming quietly to himself.

Matthew went back upstairs.

'Miss has missed the bus,' he said.

In the shouting and cheering that followed they did not notice the bus stopping. Suddenly the driver was standing at the top of the stairs.

'Quiet!'

Miss Kirk's well-trained class were silent immediately.

'You've got a choice,' the driver said. 'If you're quiet up here I won't know your teacher's missing, will I? So I can drive on as normal, can't I? If you make a racket I'll know she's not on the bus and I'll have to go back for her, won't I? Okay?'

Matthew pictured the bus reversing back to the stop, a dangerously quiet Miss Kirk getting on, the traffic jamming itself up again, Sergeant Morton getting out of his panda car and having to run over the top of all the cars to get close enough to sort it all out . . . .

'We'll be quiet,' he said, and the rest of the class nodded.

The driver went back downstairs and the bus started off again. Matthew looked behind and saw in the distance what could have been Miss Kirk waving. He waved back.

Jennifer's mum was standing at the same bus stop as they passed.

'Has she been there all the time?' Matthew asked.

'Of course not,' Jennifer said. 'She's off shopping, I expect. Oh no . . . the football shirts!'

Then she reached under her seat and pulled out the battery-bag.

'It's lucky it's the same bus,' she said, 'or I'd have lost them. Miss wouldn't have been very pleased.'

The class got off at the right stop and crocodiled tidily back to school. It made its way to its classroom and sat down quietly. Miss Kirk would have been pleased with them if she could have seen them. They all got out their books and started writing: 'Our Visit to the Museam'.

Matthew looked round. It was good to be back. He had had enough of adventures. He got up and quietly slipped the envelope back into Daniel Morton's drawer. Let him sort it out. No one could trace it to him. Now for some work to get his mind off it.

'It's a pity,' Matthew thought, 'that I can't write about the *interesting* things I saw.' He sighed and started a sentence about lamp-posts. Where was Miss Kirk, he wondered. What would she do? There wasn't another bus for an hour. Would she walk? Would she get a taxi? Sergeant Morton wasn't very likely to give her a lift after the way she had spoken to him.

It was like a Great Egg Race, Matthew thought. You leave teachers standing at bus stops. Their only equipment is a bag containing thirty clipboards. If it rained hard enough they could clip the boards together and make a raft. He pictured Miss Kirk standing rigid as a mast holding the bag up for a sail, floating down the road while the wind howled and the waves bucked her frail craft. What would they do if it didn't rain? Perhaps they should be allowed to use the contents of their handbags as well. That should give them plenty of equipment.

Just then the door opened and Miss Kirk came in looking tidy and calm. She glanced round the room, smiled, and started to write key spellings like 'museum' on the board. The clipboards looked quite dry.

As the bell for dinner play rang the door burst open and a distraught Mrs Polstead rushed in.

'Oh, Miss Kirk, I forgot the overalls. I'm so sorry. I was standing in the middle of Sainsbury's looking at the washing powder when I suddenly remembered. I'll get them done this afternoon without fail and bring them back tomorrow.'

Miss Kirk smiled graciously.

'Jennifer, give your mother the overalls, please. I'm afraid, Mrs Polstead, you'll find them rather muddy after the football yesterday.'

75

'That's all right,' Mrs Polstead replied. 'I'll give them a good hot wash. They're so big it won't matter if they shrink a bit.' She went out clutching the battery-bag.

'Books away tidily, class. First Dinners, lead out.'

Matthew rather hoped Miss Kirk would call him back. Her silence was a bit worrying. She wouldn't forget it and he'd rather get it over with. Oh well, he was used to being told off. At least things couldn't get any worse.

7
On the Mozart Trail

Miss Kirk called Matthew back at the end of afternoon school.

'I think we need to have a little talk,' she said. Matthew's heart sank. He knew who would be doing the talking. 'You have been mixed up with too many incidents over the past few days. Now, I am just going to check the computer room and then I shall come and hear what you have to say.'

Miss Kirk walked purposefully out of the classroom. Matthew stood, rooted to the spot. He had no explanations. It was all accident, and hurry, and forgetfulness, and worry about earlier disasters. But it had built up until it looked very bad. Various possibilities ran through his panicking mind.

SCENE ONE
Enter Miss Kirk

MISS KIRK: Well, Matthew.

(*Matthew throws himself on the floor at her feet and sobs*)

MATTHEW: Oh, Miss, Miss. Only you can help me. I am starved and beaten at home. I am locked in a dark cupboard all night. I am cracking up. All those crimes were a desperate cry for help.

MISS KIRK: How brave you are, Matthew, to come to school at all, and to come looking so cheerful . . . . Think no more about these minor upsets.

But Miss Kirk was more likely to tell him to get off the floor before he got his jersey dirty.

SCENE TWO
Enter Miss Kirk
MISS KIRK: Well, Matthew.
MATTHEW (*Speaking quietly and with confidence*): I have to tell you, Miss Kirk, that you have been chosen as a test subject for the new bag offensive. The High Bag Command have planned a series of experiments to see how long humans can hold out against their new

undercover techniques. They have perfected a way of making the insides of bags change places so that people will never trust bags again and they will be freed from their slavery. He did expect to have to work on you for more than three days . . . .

But Miss Kirk would say, 'What a lovely story, Matthew. Perhaps you would like to write it out for me this evening. It would take at least four sides, I think.'

SCENE THREE
Enter Miss Kirk

MISS KIRK: Well, Matthew.
MATTHEW (*standing up straight and speaking fearlessly*): You are quite right, Miss Kirk. I have been deliberately persecuting you. I swore revenge when you let Mary take the hamster home at half-term when it was my turn. I am guilty. Lead me to the Head.

But Miss Kirk actually came back into the

classroom saying: 'Matthew, have you seen my Mozart cassette box?'

Matthew thought he was dreaming. They were supposed to be discussing the Mystery of the Exchanging Bags, not a cassette box. Surely boxes hadn't joined in now? Then he remembered Saturday. The jumble sale. The Mozart symphony.

'Mozart cassette box, Miss?'

Miss Kirk sighed her well-I-suppose-I-am-actually-paid-to-put-up-with-complete-idiots-like-this sigh.

'Yes, Matthew. On Friday evening I was working on the computer. I like to play some soothing music while I use it. When I finished I must have put the computer cassette and the music cassette in the wrong boxes. Here's the Mozart in my computer box, but the other one seems to be missing.'

Was Miss Kirk the thief? Was she the brain behind an international gang of criminals and was Bainton Road Junior School the H.Q.? Would a dozen burly men burst in at any moment and torture him until he confessed

81

all? Perhaps Miss Kirk was just the record-keeper and the Head was the mastermind. That would explain why her head never quite mastered who was who in the school.

'Well, have you, Matthew?'

'What was on it, Miss?'

She suddenly smiled and sat down. 'It's funny, really. The local teachers' group is planning some Open Days so that parents can see the schools' computers working. The idea is to get them keen so that we can raise more money. We were planning out when was best to hold them, and what schools could lend what. It got a bit complicated with all the thefts there've been. I was working it all out on the computer, to show that it was of practical use. That's why I needed the Mozart, to keep me calm.'

No international gang. No mastermind. No problem.

'I did see a Mozart cassette, Miss. It was in the jumble sale.'

'Oh, no!' Miss Kirk said. 'I must have dropped it into that box of jumble that Jennifer brought. Did you see anyone buy it?'

'It was on the table when I left,' said Matthew truthfully, but not the-whole-truth-and-nothing-but-the-truthfully.

'Thanks, Matthew. I'd better go round to Mrs Kinglock straight away and see if she remembers what happened to it. I only hope some idiot hasn't recorded over the top of it.'

'But you wanted to talk to me, Miss,' said Matthew, feeling he'd rather get the Great Investigation into Buses and Bags over with now rather than have to face it in the morning.

'No, I'm sure it's just a lot of coincidences really,' she said. 'Run along now—and keep away from bags!'

Matthew ran along, and into the Head.

'Ah, Matthew. Walk now, please.'

Matthew stood looking after her with his mouth open as she walked away from him down the corridor. She knew his name! Then he shrugged. It must be another coincidence. She was bound to call him Matthew sooner or later. She'd called him everything else.

Then Matthew ran out of school and down the drive. He'd remembered the copy of the cassette he'd made for the police. Could he get it off Daniel before he gave it to his dad? If only Miss Kirk hadn't kept him back . . . but if she hadn't he wouldn't have known . . . but he would have been able to catch Daniel . . . .

Matthew paused outside the police station. He pretended to read the Wanted posters. He could make up a better one:

WANTED
Time machine to
travel back to
Friday. Return
Monday.

Then the police-station door opened and Daniel came out.

'Hi, Matthew,' he said. 'Come to give yourself up?'

'What—what are you doing here?'

'Come to see my dad, of course. There was a message for him in my drawer at school. I've just brought it for him.'

'Is he in?'

'You do want to give yourself up! No, he's out at the museum. Someone pinched some stuff while the alarm system was out of order. There's a big panic on. Anyway—what *are* you doing here?'

Inspiration struck Matthew. 'The Head asked me to give him a message about the

Green Cross Code, about talking to the school.'

'Poor Dad,' said Daniel. 'He hates doing that.'

'I'd better leave the message anyway,' said Matthew. He went through the door and up into the entrance hall. There was nobody there but on the counter was an envelope, the envelope.

Matthew stretched out one hopeful hand. He picked the envelope up and turned to walk out again. The door opened and Sergeant Morton walked in.

'Hello, Matthew. That for me, is it? Thanks.'

Matthew walked out. He had no envelope in his hand. He had not given the Head's message. He could not go back in now.

'Hey, Matthew,' Jennifer called. 'Have you seen your picture in the evening paper? You do look funny. You should have tucked the painting overall in like everyone else.'

Matthew looked in horror at the front page. There he was, an embarrassed look on his

face, painting overall to his knees.

'THE ARTFUL DODGER' the caption said.

'You'd better take a copy home to your mum,' Jennifer said. 'I'll bring one to school tomorrow. I expect Miss will pin it up.

See you!'

Matthew was not looking forward to Tuesday morning.

8
Short and to the Point

It wasn't until Assembly on Tuesday morning that things began to look rather worrying. Morning had broken again and they were sitting down ready to listen to the Head when Jennifer's mother burst into the hall.

'Ah, Mrs Polstead! We are always pleased to see parents at our Assemblies. A chair for Mrs Polstead, please.'

'No, it's not that. I mean, I can't stay. Oh, it's awful.'

Matthew glanced at Jennifer and felt almost sorry for her. When he saw what Mrs Polstead was carrying a terrible foreboding filled him. Mrs Polstead was carrying a battery-bag. But which battery-bag had she got? His question was soon answered as she slowly unzipped it and drew out a brand-new, unworn football shirt.

'Ah,' said the Head, 'the new football shirts, splendid. I believe the photographer is coming to school this morning to photograph the team . . . .'

'Stop!' cried Mrs Polstead. 'It's awful!'

'Awful?' said the Head. 'I think it's splendid publicity for the school and all the hard work the P.T.A. do.'

'But they've shrunk!' shrieked Mrs Polstead in desperation. 'They're too small. They won't fit. I've ruined them. I thought they were dirty painting overalls. I gave them the hottest wash. They're useless. They're a waste of money. They're too small.'

The Head smiled down kindly. 'My dear Mrs Polstead, what beautifully clean football shirts. Could we have the eleven youngest Infants on the stage, please.'

The Infant teachers pushed eleven reluctant midgets on to the stage. Three of them were crying already.

'Aren't they dear little things,' cooed the Head. 'Now then, dears, just put these on.'

The football shirts fitted the eleven youngest Infants perfectly. It was perhaps bad luck that nine of them were girls.

'Miss Kirk, please take the Infants' Football

Team out to be photographed,' said the Head.

Miss Kirk led the dear little things out and took a dazed Mrs Polstead with her. The Head turned to the school. 'Now you can see the way in which things so often turn out for the best. Why should the oldest children have all the best things?'

Miss Kirk put her head round the door. 'Sergeant Morton's here.'

'Ah, splendid! Come along, Sergeant. Now children, you are going to have a treat.

Sergeant Morton has come to talk to you.'

Sergeant Morton looked puzzled. He had not received the Head's message about the Green Cross Code. Matthew edged down in his place, hoping to avoid trouble.

'No,' said Sergeant Morton, 'I've just come with this computer cassette that seems to have been handed in. It was in an envelope addressed to the school. It had something stuck on the outside but that seems to have come off.'

'That's mine,' said Miss Kirk from her position half round the door. 'Thank you very much.'

'Thank you, Sergeant,' said the Head. 'Now children, sit still while the Sergeant speaks to you.'

Sergeant Moreton saw he would not be able to escape without saying something. 'You will be glad to hear,' he said, 'that we have at last caught the local computer thief.'

Matthew glanced at Miss Kirk, but she wasn't wearing handcuffs.

'The museum was robbed yesterday while

the alarm system was being reset. I think some of you know something about that. Anyway, we caught the thief quite easily. He had taken his shoes off so that he could tiptoe out without making any noise. He stepped on some broken glass in the entrance hall near the display case and left a trail of bloody footprints all the way to his car. A traffic warden had noted its number as it had helped cause a traffic jam that had built up when a bus stopped too long at Museum Street. When we went to his house we recovered the items stolen from the museum and all the missing computers. So, it's an ill wind . . . .'

Matthew thought of the trail of events that had led to him being the person really responsible for catching the computer thief. But he couldn't claim the glory. It would mean admitting too much. Better not let the cat out of the bag.

Other Titles in Andersen Young Readers' Library